SAILOR'S Night Before Christmas

SAILOR'S Night Before Christmas

Written by Kimbra Cutlip
Illustrated by James Rice

PELICAN PUBLISHING COMPANY
Gretna 1999

For Sienna, with special thanks to Michael and my mom and dad

The word "Pelican" and the depiction of a pelican are trademarks of Pelican Publishing Company, Inc., and are registered in the U.S. Patent and Trademark Office.

Library of Congress Cataloging-in-Publication Data

Cutlip, Kimbra L.
   Sailor's night before Christmas / written by Kimbra L. Cutlip ;
illustrated by James Rice
      p. cm.
   SUMMARY: In this parody of the famous poem by Clement C. Moore,
Santa Claus is a salty sailor who pays a visit to those on board a
ship in Fisherman's Bay on Christmas Eve.
   ISBN 1-56554-395-5
   1. Santa Claus Juvenile poetry. 2. Christmas Juvenile poetry. 3.
Sailors Juvenile poetry. 4. Children's poetry, American. [1. Santa
Claus Poetry. 2. Christmas Poetry. 3. Sailors Poetry. 4. American
poetry. 5. Narrative poetry.] I. Rice, James, 1934 - ill. II. Title.
   PS3553.U845 S25 1999

                                                             99-30579
                                                                  CIP

Printed in Korea

Published by Pelican Publishing Company, Inc.
1000 Burmaster Street, Gretna, Louisiana 70053

Sailor's Night Before Christmas

'Twar the night a'fore Christmas on Fisherman's Bay,
And the wind she war calm, like she had been all day.

The sails they war stowed an' the sea war like glass,
But the red sky that morn' told me it wouldn't last.

The youngin's war snorin', a whistlin', an' sleepin,
Dreamin' o' porpoises dancin' an' leapin'.

The capt'n, 'e'd dogged all the hatches down tight,
An' swashed down the last o' the chowder in sight.
'E grumbled out "arrrrg" as 'e blew out the light,
An' I, the first mate, took me watch fer the night.

Wit me sights firmly trained on the stars in the sky,
I might 'ave just blinked wit me only good eye.
When shiver me timbers the wind took a swing,
An' raged from the north like a fierce howlin' thing.

I sprang up the riggin' to better me view.
Wit me sight-glass in hand, I could see whar she blew.
Thar, like a whale comin' full to the breech,
I saw the sea break an' I 'erd the wind screech.

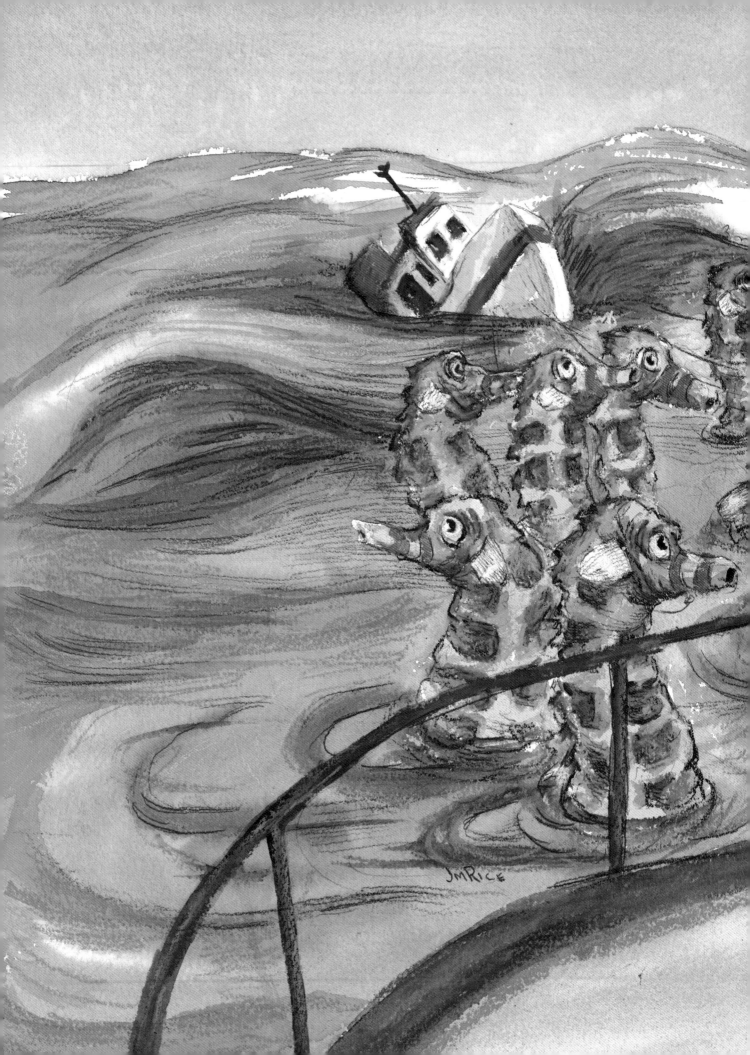

As a wave crashed down on us, I squinted to see,
Eight giant seahorses haul a tug from the sea.
I let go me grip on the tarry ol' mast,
An' nearly fell o'er the rail in the blast.

Aye now me matey, I knows what yer thinkin',
But I'd barely been noddin', an' I sure I warn't drinkin'.
Wipin' salt from me eyes, I rechecked agin,
There'd be no mistakin' this warn't just a wind.

Me mammy she'd told me o' just such a sight,
An ol' Capt'n Clause who come hauntin' at night.

Chock full o' glitterin' chandlery toys,
That wee tug she blew 'er foghorn o'er the noise.
The wind called each seahorse by name like it knew,
While the wave they war surfin' headed straight fer ar crew.

"Yo Trawler, Yo Schooner, Yo Cutter, an' Clipper,
Ho Bosun, Ho Coxswain, Ho Matey, an' Skipper."

From the decks, up the mast, to the bowsprit they played.
An' ar vessel she rocked port to starboard unstayed.

In a blink the queer squall come abrupt to a halt,
An' thar on ar deck come to rest the ol' salt.

I ducked down below, my head spun 'round.
An' thar through the hatch come ol' Clause wit a bound.

'E smelled like a tide gone too long from the shore,
An' 'e stood in the cabin drippin' o'er the floor,
Red tailcoat, red kerchief, black boots, an' black belt,
An' thar in 'is pockets, leapin' minnows an' smelt.

Wit 'is big rounded belly 'e stood soakin' wet,
An' rolled from 'is shoulder a fishermen's net,
Stuffed full o' treasures I'd ne'r seen a'fore,
An' toys fer the young lads, the ship's cat, an' more.

The ol' man war swift as 'e tended 'is duty,
Stuffin' ar ditty bags full up wit booty.
'Is load heeled the boat way o'er to one side,
An' I laughed just to meet a sea capt'n so wide.

'Is red face it shone like the skin o' a fish.
Then the sot grumbled past me, "ARRRRG, make a wish."
The smoke from 'is pipe filled the boat like a cloud,
An' I followed 'im coughin' an' hackin' out loud.

Straight to the galley 'e swaggered headstrong,
Fer a swig o' ar coffee, an' a biscuit, an' song.
Through 'is matted white beard, 'e chortled a toon,
Somethin' 'bout lists 'e'd been checkin' since noon.
Then, certain 'e'd done what 'e come here to do,
'E downed the last cup, nodded once, an' war through.

Wit a wink, an' a grumble, an' a puff o' 'is pipe,
'E bound out the hatch straight into the night.
Two toots o' 'is horn an' those seahorses jolted.
To windward 'is tug an' it's cargo they bolted.

But I heard 'im hollar as they sailed outta sight,
"Yo Ho Ho an' a tide full o' Yule,
Merry Christmas, ya lubbers,
Have yeself a good night."